Once Upon a Fairy Tale

Shirl Knobloch

• • •

Once Upon a Fairy Tale

© Shirley Knobloch, 2015

Edited by: Jennifer Sabatelli

Cover and Photography by: Shirl Knobloch

ISBN 13: 978-0-9885171-8-9

Also by Shirl Knobloch:

- *Birdsong, Barks, and Banter: Adventures of an Animal Intuitive Reiki Master and Her Home of Misfit Companions*

- *The Returning Ones: A Medium's Memoirs*

- *You're Never Too Old for Fairy Tales*

- *Reenactments from My Heart: Spiritual and Supernatural Civil War Fiction and Poetry*

• • •

"A children's story that can only be enjoyed by children is not a good children's story in the slightest."
— C.S. Lewis

• • •

...

Table of Contents

• • •

• • •

Prologue

I wrote my first book of fairy tales with the intent of reaching both young and old, adding a bit of whimsy and "once upon a time" to those whose lives had seen too much sorrow. When I started hearing back from readers, I knew I had accomplished that feat. Some wrote to tell me they read a story before bed, preferring to drift off to sleep peacefully, rather than in a state of agitation after the evening news. Most savored the book slowly, reading one fairy tale at a sitting.

My most cherished letter came from a reader who shared my book with her elderly mother, both of them reading to each other. So the wheel of life had turned full cycle. The happiness of childhood fairy tales had now become the final, treasured moments between a daughter and a mother near the end of her life.

I hope those who enjoyed the journey through my first book will continue on and enjoy the next path. My first book cover showed the doorway upon which to enter. This one shows the entire castle, beckoning those to continue on to a place of *once upon a time.*

Enjoy the journey, for it is true—you can return home to a time of fairy tales.

The Leaf Who Longed to Dance

Once upon a time, in a forest of tall trees and dark shadows, there grew a tiny leaf. She was beautiful, her green gown shimmering in the morning sun, the tips of her leafy hem pointing up toward the sky.

Day after day, she listened to the wind singing through the branches and longed to dance. She curled her leafy tips into the prettiest pliés; but, try as she might, she could not leap into the air and dance.

She asked the little birds who flew by, "Can you dance?" The little birds dove and dipped in the sky, fluttering their wings and twirling their feathers in the wind, but all little leaf could do was watch.

She asked the teensy spiders, "Can you dance?" The spiders spun sparkling webs that filled with dew as they glided across the threads on eight graceful legs before her. Little leaf watched in sadness. She wanted to twirl in the wind; she wanted to glide on sparkly threads of silver.

Time passed. Little leaf practiced every day, pointing her tips and curling her soft skin. "I must keep practicing. One day I will dance on the wind," she cried. The other leaves teased her. "We are leaves," they laughed. "We do not dance!!!"

Months passed. Many forest beings passed along her branch, and each little creature told her how they danced in the wind. Squirrel grabbed the branches and danced from tree to tree, never missing a step. Hawk moved his wings ever so slightly and let the wind carry him in a wondrous waltz. Some creatures danced on the ground. The deer pranced and hopped among the tall grass. The chipmunks scurried among the shadows. The crickets tapped their legs together in a nightly quick step.

But little leaf didn't dance. Each day, the sun rose and her leaf tips were still. Each night, she closed her eyes in uneasy rest and dreamed of whirling through the sky.

Months passed again. Little leaf felt odd. Her beautiful green gown was burnished into a lovely shade of gold by the autumn sun. Age had crinkled her skin a bit, but she grew more beautiful with each passing day.

Other leaves around her were changing too. They were very frightened. Little leaf wasn't frightened, though. Somehow, she knew this was right. "Don't worry, we are all going to dance." She comforted those around her, those who had laughed and mocked her so many days of the passing seasons. "We cannot dance!" they cried. One by one, they fell to the ground. Only little leaf was left. She did not lose faith. She knew she was going to dance.

And dance she did! A great gust of wind blew through the branches. It caught her leaf points and carried her, soaring into the sky. She twirled and pliéd. She danced for the squirrels, for the spiders, for the hawk, for the chipmunk, and for the deer. They clapped their paws and entwined their legs in applause. It was the most beautiful dance they had ever seen. Little leaf was so graceful; she let the wind lead and was the most enchanting partner he had ever carried off to dance in the sky.

When the dance was over, wind gently used his breath to carry her softly down to the ground. Little leaf was exhausted but happier than she had ever been. She slowly shut her eyes and drifted off to peaceful slumber.

Pure of Heart

*I*n a kingdom far away and long, long ago lived a brave king and his kind-hearted son.

The little prince would wander away from his nurse each day and visit the grave of his mother, the Queen. She had been killed in a terrible battle; the knights of the kingdom had fought valiantly but could not protect her from harm.

"One day, my son, you shall become a brave knight," the king told his son. "But some years must pass before then—not many, though, for I am growing old."

The kingdom was a much more peaceful place now. The only fear was of dragons that lived among the caves that bordered the sea. The Prince was told never to wander that far, to stay within the castle lands.

But sometimes little princes do not listen, for adventure and mischief overrule the wishes of a drowsy nurse who falls into slumber in the afternoon sun. The prince walked along the caves, exploring the rocks and seashells until he heard a mournful cry.

This was a very kind prince; he loved all the creatures of the castle lands. He walked toward the cries. Entangled in a large and thorny briar bush was a baby dragon. He had never seen a dragon before. This one did not look frightening. The baby's eyes looked up at the Prince, pleading for help.

The Prince had been taught never to touch a dragon; one touch and their poisonous scales can kill you. Their breath of fire can burn your skin. Their treacherous teeth can shred your skin.

The Prince didn't think of teeth, of dragon breath, of poison; he only thought of the little baby's eyes and the torn cuts on his skin from the briar thorns. He took out the little pocket knife his father had given him and slowly cut away the branches.

Now, from a high cliff, mother dragon was watching, waiting to harm whoever hurt her son. She had tried to free him, but her talons were too big to grab the tiny branches. She could not burn them away with her fire breath because her baby would be burned as well. So she watched in agony as he struggled to be free—that is, until the kind prince came.

Soon, the Prince had cut each thorn away, and the little baby was free. No breath of fire came from the little mouth, only a green tongue that licked the boy from head to toe.

The Prince giggled. He swore never to hurt a dragon for the rest of his life. He walked with the baby to the edge of the sea and dabbed some water on his wounds. Dragon wounds don't hurt with salt water; they heal. All the while, the mother watched. She feared man. They hated her kind; they only sought to kill them, not help them. *Who was this kind human*, she wondered. Swooping down from the cliff, she flew down to the shore.

The boy had never seen a dragon, only read of them in storybooks and heard what the knights had to say about their evilness. He was terrified. The baby cried in happiness and ran to his mother's side. She spread her huge wings around him and spoke. "You helped my son, do not fear. You are safe from dragons from this day forward. Speak your name, and I shall tell all dragons of this Realm to never harm thee."

"I am Prince William."

Hearing that, the mother dragon winced. She knew the legends. She knew the future awaiting William. First, he must become a knight. And to become a knight, a dragon must be slain at his hand. The mark of a king's true courage and heart was to be a dragon slayer. Mother Dragon bid him farewell. She knew their time as friends was over.

Years passed. Prince William grew into a young man, and the King grew elderly and frail.

"It is time for you to become a knight, my son. The other knights will teach you how to fight and kill. There is the test you must pass before I give my Realm to you."

"What test, Father?" asked William.

"You must slay a dragon. Only the pure of heart can slay a dragon."

Prince William's heart sank deep within his chest. He could not disappoint his father, but he would not kill a dragon either. Silently, he left his father's bedside and left to join the knights. They taught him jousting, sword fighting, and weaponry. They taught him of honor, courage, and chivalry. Most of all, they taught him of the toxins of dragons, of the fire breath of dragons, of the jagged talons of dragons, and of the evil of these beings.

Months passed, and it was time. Suited in armor and carrying a newly forged sword, Prince William set out on a quest, the quest to bring back the heart of a dragon. Dragon hearts were made of pure garnet. Only a few knights had ever carried one back to the Kingdom, where they gleamed in glass cases in the knight's chamber.

The quest was a solitary one, and William's mind replayed the day years before when he touched a tiny dragon and it licked him to return his kindness.

William decided to leave the kingdom. The King would think he died, and another would be chosen to rule. It was the only choice he could make—he would not harm a dragon. He walked to the seaside, searching the cliffs to catch a glimpse of his friend, but the skies were silent. William came upon a cave to shelter him for the night. Inside, he heard faint cries. He followed the sound and came upon a large dragon, lying on its side.

"Prince William, I have been waiting to meet you again. I am the mother dragon whose baby you saved so many years before. I am old and sick now; soon, it will be my time to leave this Realm forever. Stay with me, for I do not wish to die alone. When I die, I will give you my heart."

Prince William stayed, not because he wanted her heart, but because she was his friend. He brought her water, he laid his tiny blanket down for her head to rest upon, and he told her stories of his home.

Her sighs grew fainter; her breath came slower; her head lifted less often. "I leave soon, William. Promise me you will take my heart. You will be a brave knight and a kind king. Tell everyone in your kingdom never to harm my kind anymore. Tell them we are not evil. Tell them we only wish to live in peace with our children."

With those words, she took her final breath. With all of her final strength, she raised her huge talon and cut a slit down her chest of scales. A beautiful garnet gleamed in the sunlight that shone down through a crack in the cave's ceiling. Prince William gently lifted the garnet and wrapped it within his tiny blanket. He could not bury his friend, but he searched the cliff side until he found a bush of beautiful roses and laid them at her side. Sadly, he made his way home.

Much time had passed. The King was dying. Everyone thought the Prince had died as well. All were surprised to see his walk inside the castle. At his father's bedside, William unwrapped the blanket. His father saw the garnet, and a peaceful expression shone through his eyes. "My brave son, now you will rule." With that, his eyes shut.

King William did rule. His first edict was the banishment of dragon slaying from the kingdom. No more stories of their evilness would be permitted; they would be safe. All the garnet hearts were taken from the glass cases and buried among the cliff sides where the dragons dwelled. Among the cliffs, beautiful roses now grew—deep red, the color of garnets.

Prince William ruled for many decades. Courage was truly in those who were pure of heart.

The Wishing Tree

*T*his is the story of a great tree. The tallest of trees, she towered among the others in the forest. She had lived for centuries and centuries and was wiser than all the trees around her. They called her Mother and looked to her for wisdom and guidance in all things.

The people in the nearby village looked upon her with awe as well. So massive was her trunk, so high were her branches, she seemed to grow right into heaven. And so she became their doorway to heaven. She became their wishing tree.

The villagers wished for many things. Some wanted love; most wished for money. They tried to hang ribbons and gifts on Mother Tree's branches, but they were too high. So they began driving little nails into her trunk, hanging ribbons. Gold ribbons wished for wealth, red ribbons for the heart's wishes. At first, Mother Tree didn't mind. She used her wisdom and guidance to help each one.

Soon, though, news spread around the villages of Mother Tree's magick. Hundreds came. They walked, rode in wagons and carts, or came on horseback, all to have wishes fulfilled.

So many spikes, so many wounds; Mother Tree could not bear the pain each day. She would cry tears of sap during the night. All was still except for the weeping of Mother Tree. And all the other trees listened and cried for their Mother.

Mother Tree lost all her strength. Her beautiful branches grew dry and brittle. Her leaves began to fall to the earth. Her trunk withered and died.

Most of the village people left, too frightened to stay. They searched the land for another wishing tree. Only a few old villagers remained. And it is their story that I now tell.

Soon after the wishing tree died, a strange thing happened in the forest. The other trees began to change color. Their leaves turned red and gold, the colors of the wishing tree's ribbons. Soon after, each leaf fell to the ground. We were very afraid but too old to journey elsewhere. We thought all the trees were gone. It was a very hard winter. We helped one another survive, sharing all we had and not placing riches over friendship and love.

It was too cold to venture out to the forest until the harsh season ended. Then the snow began to melt. We walked among the tall trees and saw the remains of hundreds and hundreds of scattered ribbons. Ribbons that meant so much at one time, that meant nothing to us now. We needed food. We needed our trees that gave us nuts and fruits and sheltered us from harsh winds. Without them, we could not live.

We gathered up all the ribbon scraps and wove them into a beautiful wreath. We placed that wreath at Mother Tree's lifeless trunk, so sorry for what we had done.

At that moment, we heard a sigh. Perhaps it was the wind; we were old, and our hearing wasn't as sharp as in our younger years. But the sigh seemed to come from all directions, from all the bare trees that shadowed our path. In an instant, green leaves replaced their emptiness. Apples and peaches hung heavy on their branches. Apples of red and peaches of gold—the real treasures, we now realized.

We told no one of this. The others in search of their wishing trees must learn the lessons themselves when they too become old and wise.

Fairy Graves

A cluster of wildflowers

Close to the ground

Might cover the place

Of a burial mound

Stones sculpted in cairns

A rock carved into a heart

Might signal the spot

Where a fairy did part

So if you see blossoms

In a quiet patch of field

Where the dew always sparkles

And the sun

Never shields

You just might be passing

A place of great grace

And if you look closely

Might glimpse fairy's face

The fairies bring flowers

They build the stone mounds

They weep at the gravesites

They honor the grounds

Leave blossoms untainted

Cairns do not disarray

For the fairies are watching

Each night and each day

The Little Dog's Warm Heart

In a castle woodland, there lived a kind little dog and the gentle woman who loved him. He was a tiny dog, but his heart was filled with kindness for all beings. She was a gentle soul, a baker for the King. Together, they shared a modest cottage at the edge of the woods.

Each day, the old baker woman would set out for work in the early morning hours and bid her furry friend farewell. Early each evening, her tired feet would walk home, and she would carry leftover scraps of madeleines and gingerbread men and sugar cookies for the tiny dog to have as treats.

Food was modest, but they always had enough. There was enough for the two of them and enough to share. So share they did. They left crumbs for the birds each morning and bowls for the feral cats and stray dogs of the kingdom. They carried vegetable scraps on walks for the geese and swans.

Little dog always carried his cookies off to his bed and tucked them under his blanket. He had many, many blankets. The baker loved to knit; she made him blankets and sweaters of every color, asking the castle seamstress to save her all scraps of yarn.

Little dog's cookies would always be gone from his bed. The baker woman thought he finished them as a late snack until one day, his secret was revealed. As she set off for work, she realized she had forgotten her shawl. The morning air was brisk, and her aging bones were chilled. She set back on the path for home again. When she arrived at the edge of the clearing, a surprising sight awaited her eyes.

She saw little dog pushing a large gingerbread man through his doggy door. She saw several feral cats and stray dogs waiting. As she watched them share a morning treat, her eyes misted with water. *Such a kind little dog, I shall have to save more scraps each day for him*, she thought. Her heart so warmed, she didn't need her shawl after all, and she turned around for work.

Thankfully, she made it home before the real cold set in. It was a harsh winter; snow was abundant and the ground was frozen solid. Now, more than ever, the beings of the woodland depended on the kind little dog and his loving companion. Crumbs were left at birdhouses, and bowls of food and water were set upon the snow.

Little dog began acting oddly. He did not wait for cookies any longer. His coughing filled the night. Baker woman was very worried. She told the castle doctor about her little boy. One night, he drove the old woman home in his carriage and examined the little dog.

"He is not well. I am sorry that his time here grows very short," he sadly told her. "It is his heart. I am sad that there is not much I can do, except ease the coughing a bit for him."

The little dog looked up at the castle doctor with large, grateful eyes. He curled up in a ball in his bed as the baker woman wrapped a soft blanket around him. She hated leaving him each day for work, and she hurried home as fast as her old legs would carry her in the snow.

Her own heart was worried. The ground was so frozen and covered with snow—how could she lay her friend to rest? She did not have the strength for this task. She prayed he would live to see the spring.

Sick as he was, the tiny dog still carried treats out to his friends each morning. They knew their friend was dying; they could see the glimmer fading from his coat and eyes.

One morning, he carried all the treats from his cookie jars, all the blankets the baker woman had knitted, and all the sweaters she had made for him. He made many trips through his doggy door, his tired heart filled with determination. One by one, he handed them to his friends. The feral cats felt warm for the first time in many months. The tiny dogs snuggled into sweaters, the large dogs wrapped soft blankets around them. The winter birds and squirrels carried pieces of cookies into their nests. The swans and geese carried off bits of yarn to keep their babies warm.

The following morning, he did not stir from his bed. His breath was very shallow, and his eyes only opened for a moment to say good morning to the old woman he loved.

The baker did not go to the castle on this day. Her heart felt very heavy as she watched a fresh snowfall cover the white ground of her garden. Then, she saw a bewildering sight! Feral cats and stray dogs came to the garden, their heads bowed and paws clasped as if in prayer.

They were in prayer! They were praying for their friend. Each was wearing a colorful sweater, one of the sweaters she had knitted! The birds came, the squirrels, the swans, the geese, all praying for her little boy.

She went over to the little dog's bed and gently picked him up in her arms. She carried him to the window as the morning sun streamed in. The little dog opened his eyes and looked out upon his friends. He gave a tiny bark and fell into peaceful, final slumber.

The baker woman wrapped him in her finest blanket and carried him outside. She laid him on the snow and worried how she would find the strength to bury her friend. As all their forest friends gathered round, the snow under the tiny dog began to melt. His kind heart had filled the spot with warmth, and all snow disappeared, revealing soft ground.

The baker woman dug with her garden spade, the feral cats clawed, and the stray dogs used their paws as shovels. Together, they dug a grave for the little dog.

From that day onward, there was always a cookie and bowl of food at the spot. It is said that at the edge of the woodland, to this day, there is a tiny patch of ground where the snow never sticks and always melts when hitting the ground. That is because it is the site of a little dog's warm heart.

True Beauty

nce upon a time there lived a homely little child. Her parents were poor, and their hopes of raising a beautiful daughter to attract a wealthy prince were soon dashed as the years revealed a plain mouse of a child. Julia was quiet; she read books, walked in the forest, and shunned parties and fancy clothes for the woodlands and peasant frocks.

The other village children made fun of Julia. They made fun of her clothes, of her hair, of her quiet ways. No one understood how truly special she was. Julia could sit in the forest and talk to the birds, chat with the fawns, laugh with the foxes. She knew all their languages; she spoke to them through her heart.

One day, a very old crone met Julia in the forest. "Would you like to be beautiful, my child?" asked the crone. "Would you like all the children to envy you, for all the village boys to fight for your affections?"

Julia thought for a moment. How nice it would be not to be made fun of, to feel like all the others, to be understood. Imagine how proud her parents might be.

"There is just one thing," whispered the crone. "In return, I wish the gift of your heart. You will lose your gift to speak with the squirrels, sing with the birds, laugh with the foxes. I have watched you, my child. Give me your gift, and I will give you beauty, riches, and friends who lay praises at your feet."

Julia accepted. Each day brought more glimmer to Julia's hair, more sparkle to her eyes. The boys who jeered now tried to steal kisses from her beautiful lips. Invitations to balls started coming to her parents' door. Princes were sending servants to find out who the new village beauty could be.

But Julia was never so sad. She missed the song of birds; she missed the laughter of foxes; she felt lost without the friendship of all the woodland creatures. In despair, Julia sought out the old crone, but she was nowhere to be found.

Then, Julia found a young girl sitting on the edge of the woodlands, singing with the birds. Something about the girl's eyes was familiar, something in her voice, though more youthful now.

"It IS you!" she cried. "Please take my beauty and give me back my heart."

The old crone gazed mournfully at the girl. "Once you give your heart, it can never be returned. You possessed more than you ever imagined, my child. Now, it is lost."

Julia tried to speak to the birds; they flew away in fright. She tried to laugh with the foxes; they dashed off into the woods.   She tried to play with the squirrels; they scampered up to the highest branches.

Julia went home.   Tears soaked through the gilded invitations on her bed. Julia lived a life of loneliness. In time, she became an old crone. Her parents died, her suitors found others to marry, and Julia was alone. Villagers often heard her calling to the birds, walking by herself on the path to her secluded cottage each day.

Mouse Shoes

Once there was a little mouse who longed for a pair of sparkly shoes. From her tiny chair, Elsa would peer through her mouse hole and see the shoes of the palace adorn the royal family's court. There were satin slippers with delicate embroidery, jeweled heels, and buckled patent leathers.

Tiny Elsa looked down at her bare feet and wished for a pair of shoes. At night when all were sleeping, she would creep into the Queen's chamber, climb into her dancing shoes, and pretend to glide across the floor, arm in arm with a handsome mouse. But all the shoes were very big, quite larger than her little mouse body.

"Oh," she cried. "I shall never have a pretty pair of shoes."

Her parents didn't understand. "We can't wear shoes," they said. "We have to be very quiet, on our toes, so humans don't hear us."

But, day after day, little Elsa sat and watched as feet went by in pretty shoes. Red shoes, brown shoes, shoes of every color. Cloth shoes, leather shoes, shoes of every shape. "One day, I shall have a beautiful pair of shoes!" she exclaimed. "Then I shall dance across our mouse home and kick my mice feet in the air!"

Soon, it was time for little mouse to take a beau. "The mouse who brings me shoes will win my heart," she declared. As she was quite lovely, several mice set out on their shoe quests. But, unlike Cinderella's circumstances, all the shoes were too big!

"Let us make a shoe our home," one little mouse pleaded to Elsa on bended mouse knee.

"No!!! I don't want to live in a shoe. I want a pretty pair to wear on my mice feet!!!"

Finally, one brave little mouse had an idea. Simon ventured into a part of the castle all mice feared. Everyone knew to stay away from the bedroom of the little Princess. Fear of mice in her room made all keep guard against the appearance of these little beings. The King's cat kept fierce watch on the Princess. No mouse dare enter her room for fear it would be his last adventure on earth.

Simon crept quietly in. So many shadows! A monstrous bear sat on the floor, casting a frightful shadow on the wall. A horse sat quite still in the corner. Then, Simon spotted a tiny house. Upon closer investigation, he found tiny furniture inside and tiny people his own size! There were fathers and mothers and children, and each wore a delicately fashioned pair of shoes.

"Oh," he cried. "This pair would be perfect for Elsa."

Suddenly, he heard the sound of cat paws on the floor. Shaking, Simon hid behind a curtain in one of the windows of the miniature house. He hardly breathed, knowing that with one pounce he would be done for. Luckily, the cat was distracted by another sound in the castle.

Simon quickly started chewing at the buttons and undid their threads. He tugged and tugged and finally loosened the pair of soft slippers from the doll's feet. A sparkling crystal blossom adorned the front of each.

Quietly, he crept back out of the nursery and down to Elsa's mouse hole. He got down on his mouse knees and held up his treasure for lovely Elsa to see.

"Oh," she gasped. "They are the most beautiful shoes I have ever seen!" She tried them on her feet. They were a perfect fit. The soft slippers made no sound as she pranced about the room. Simon took her hand and gently twirled her about the floor.

With each step, the dreams of two little mice became one, for it was Simon who had swept her off her tiny mouse feet with a beautiful pair of slippers. The sparkles on her feet were only matched by the love in Simon's eyes as he danced with his lovely bride.

The Long Flight Home

In a far off place of sand and dunes, there lived a lonely little mouse. Mouse was the only one of his kind in this place. He could not see his reflection; the only pools of water were stagnant and dirty, but he could imagine what he seemed to be.

Mouse had fleeting memories of another place, another land far away, but that was when he was just a baby. A land of forests and trees and tall, green grass. A land of sparkling, clear lakes and running streams and beautiful, red strawberries so juicy and sweet. Here, there were no strawberries, just tough weeds and brambles and scarcely enough seeds to keep a lonely little mouse alive.

There were other beings in this place, but Mouse hid from all. Some scurried in burrows, some flew through the skies, but Mouse knew he was not one of them, and so he was alone.

Once, many full and new moons ago, Mouse remembered flying through the skies. He remembered the large wings of a creature who carried him. He remembered the fear, and he remembered falling. Falling to the ground, tumbling and rolling over and over until the sand covered him and kept him safe. And there was something else, but little

Mouse could not remember it; his baby memories were very blurred.

Mouse knew he had only one ear. He felt its empty place when he rubbed his paws over his head to wash away the sand and dirt. But he was a mouse, and he could still hear all the sounds of this place with one very sharp ear and long, skillful whiskers that felt the vibrations of all who walked or crawled near.

One morning, Mouse heard the mournful cries of a being in distress. Mouse was a kind soul. The cries beckoned, and he scampered along the sand to their source. He found Raven, a large, black being who flew through the skies. Only he was not flying—in his tail were sharp quills, the quills of a large cactus.

"Please help me, Mouse," the raven cawed. "I cannot reach these quills with my beak. Without my tail feathers, I cannot fly."

Mouse was afraid of these creatures of the sky. No, he was terrified. It was one of these creatures who brought him here, carried him to these sands so far away from home. Far away from his family, far away from the trees and streams, and far away from the place he belonged.

"How do I know you will not eat me?" asked Mouse. "You have to trust me," said Raven. "Ravens never lie. Once they make a promise, a promise is kept."

Mouse, being the kind soul that he was, slowly pulled each quill from Raven's tail. One by one, he pulled until his teeth ached and his mouth grew very tired.

Raven watched this mouse in awe, not quite believing how a tiny being he would have eaten under any other circumstances was now using all of his strength to save a stranger's life. He stared into Mouse's kind eyes and saw the missing place where a furry ear would have been. A deep sadness filled Raven's body unlike any sadness he had every known.

"That is the last one," said Mouse. "The quills are all removed. You can fly." Mouse started to shake and move his tiny feet backwards, fearing the raven's attack.

"A promise was made, and a promise shall be kept," said Raven. "What may I do for you in return?" he asked the little mouse.

Mouse thought. Finally, he answered. "I want to go home. Can you take me there? It is a place of forests and streams and crystal-clear lakes. It is far away. I do not know the way. Can you find it?" he asked Raven.

"I know the place," cawed the large bird. "I will take you there. You must trust me. Do you trust me, little mouse?"

Little Mouse longed for home. His longing was stronger than any fear. "I will trust you, Raven," he replied.

Raven gathered Mouse up in his strong feet and told him to hold on tightly. Together, by the light of the full moon, they flew over mountains. They flew through the clouds; they flew with the wind; they passed over large patches of sand and grass. Then, Mouse saw the towering trees. He saw the running streams, the crystal-clear lakes. Slowly, Raven drifted down to the ground. He let Mouse down on a patch of strawberries.

"A promise is a promise, my friend," he cawed. "And most important of all, my heart is sorry," he cried as he spread his wings in the air and took off in flight.

Mouse looked up and saw a patch of white feathers on Raven's chest. Now he remembered. He remembered what he had forgotten all those moons ago. He remembered soaring in the sky below a tuft of white feathers that flew with the wind between a pair of huge, black wings. He remembered a beak tugging at his ear, trying to hold on. He remembered breaking free, falling, tumbling to the sand.

But now he was home. He was safe. Peering through the strawberry leaves, he saw tiny eyes glowing in the moonlight. The tiny eyes of his family! One by one, they scurried to give him the biggest mouse hugs a mouse can give. They stroked the empty place where his ear used to be. They asked him where he had been. A million mouse questions, but all the time in the world to answer—this night, and the next, and the night after that. The nights of all the full and new moons to come, under the trees, in the land of lakes and streams.

The Oak

O nce upon a time, in a village in a far off land, there lived a carpenter and his family. The carpenter was very gifted; he could create anything from a block of wood. Kings and princes commissioned his craft. Pieces of his furniture graced the courts of palaces near and far.

The carpenter loved his wife and children. His eldest boy loved working in his father's shop. He possessed a spirit that was at one with the pieces of wood. His name suited him perfectly—Darach, the ancient word for oak. He could feel which piece should be carved and fitted in perfect craftsmanship. Sometimes, as he carved, it was hard for his father to see where Darach's hands ended and where the wood began.

One day, sadly, his young son was helping carve in the woodworking shop when a horrible accident injured the boy's leg. The boy became very ill with infection and lay listlessly in bed for many weeks. When he became well enough, he tried to stand again, but he could not support himself on his injured leg.

Filled with grief, his father set off to find the strongest tree in the forest. Casting his eyes upon a massive oak, he chopped it down and carried a piece of its trunk back to his workshop. The carpenter began to carve a beautiful walking stick.

The top of the stick was carved into the shape of an oak leaf. Too poor to afford jewels, the carpenter searched for pieces of sparkling mica and inlaid them into the leaf to create a design of sparkling veins. So lifelike, the leaf sparkled in the sun. As he carved and polished his piece, he prayed that his creation would help Darach walk again.

The carpenter did not know that this was a very special piece of wood, taken from a dryad tree. Dryad trees possessed spirits. They held great magick and wisdom in their bark. All fairies knew this to be true and could be seen dancing among them.

When his carving was finished, the carpenter brought the walking stick to his son. "This strong oak will give you strength," he told Darach. "Upon this stick you will lean and walk again."

"How beautiful, Father. I think this is your greatest work," his son cried. Leaning on the stick, the boy stood off the bed and walked across the floor. He did not feel pain and went outside in the sunlight for the first time in many weeks.

The oak leaf sparkled in the sun. As if by magick, the boy did not feel weak any longer. It felt as if his spirit and the walking stick were one. He could feel the strength of the wood; it was as if the wood were filling his body with energy.

He would tell his father this, but his father would simply dismiss his thoughts as the imaginings of a little boy. But it was hard to see where the boy's hand ended and the oak leaf began; it truly looked as if the two had merged. The sparkling veins of the leaf seemed to flow into the veins of Darach's hand. The boy grew strong again, even stronger than before the injury.

Darach continued to help his father in his workshop, where his carving became more extraordinary with each passing day. Soon, noblemen and kings were commissioning pieces his skilled hands would create. Darach would help his father deliver finished pieces to the village noblemen. Together, father and son worked side by side, happily in their workshop among the wood they cherished.

Darach never left home without the walking stick. As he walked through the village, the noblemen eyed the boy's beautiful possession with envy. Many times, they asked him to sell it, but the boy refused. The stick was part of him; never would he walk without it.

One day, a very greedy nobleman hired a bandit to attack the carpenter's wagon and steal the walking stick from Darach. The bandit waited until the boy was alone and struck him in the head from behind. He then took off with the stick.

Returning to the wagon, Darach's father placed his unconscious boy back in the cart and returned home. Grief stricken, he carried his son into the house and into his bed. "Please do not leave me," he cried to his son. "I will craft you an even more beautiful walking stick, but I can never replace you." The boy was very still, as if the energy from his body faded with every breath.

Meanwhile, the bandit brought the treasure to the greedy nobleman. The nobleman noticed a slight limp in the bandit's leg. "What happened?" he asked.

"It's nothing. I must have injured it when I grabbed the boy off the wagon," he answered. "Just pay me my money, and I will be on my way." The nobleman paid, and the bandit hobbled off.

"Oh, what a treasure!" the nobleman rejoiced. "I shall hide you away and keep you all to myself." The nobleman took the walking stick and held it in his hands, cradling his fingers around the sparkling leaf. Never had he seen such artistry. Suddenly, a sharp pain shot down his leg. Panicked, he dropped the walking stick.

That night, the pain grew worse and worse. The nobleman took to his bed and could not lift his legs to rise again. He called his servant. "Take that evil stick! Take it back to the carpenter! It is evil magick, and I do not want it in my house."

The servant took the walking stick, but he did not return it. Instead, he ran away to the neighboring castle to sell it to the King. His thoughts swirled with greed when he thought of the price this beauty would fetch. Halfway there, he collapsed on the road, unable to take another step.

A group of fairies sat hidden, watching in the woods by the roadside. They gathered their strength and dragged the beautiful stick back to the carpenter's workshop. In a state of shock and bewilderment and grief, the carpenter picked up the walking stick and brought it to Darach's bedside. The boy still lay unconscious, but soon his eyes opened and his hands clasped the handle of the stick.

"My oak," he cried. Darach sat up, wrapped his fingers around the oak leaf, and walked from his bedroom into the afternoon sun. He walked to the edge of the woods where the giant dryad had once stood and placed the stick into the ground. Immediately, large branches twirled around it, large roots spread out into the ground. A massive trunk formed around the boy's legs and enveloped his body, reaching toward heaven.

The carpenter kept his secret. How could he explain? Instead, he told the villagers that the injury had taken Darach's life. Only his wife and other children knew, but how much they believed his story was hard to say. They dismissed it as the imaginings of a grieving father.

Seasons passed. No one touched this magical tree. Some say the oak leaves sparkled like jewels in the morning sun. Villagers called it a dryad tree, and dryad trees possess spirits. The fairies knew this to be true.

As for the carpenter, his broken heart would not allow him to carve into another tree again. He spent his remaining years alone in the woods, stopping each day by a massive oak and placing his arms around its trunk.

The Sparrow Who Longed to Read

Once upon a time, in a land filled with towers and castles, there lived a tiny sparrow. Sparrow lived in a willow tree, in a nest of thread and down feathers from the swans that lived on the palace lake.

Sparrow was a talkative bird. He could sing verses and send messages throughout the entire kingdom. Each night, he sang out the latest gossip and news from his high perch on the willow tree for all his friends to hear.

But Sparrow longed to read. He looked at castle signs and saw messengers carrying pamphlets throughout the village. *Oh, how I wish I could read*, he thought. *Then I could tell all the animals in the kingdom the news of the village.* Sparrow tried to remember the letters. He practiced writing them with his beak in the dirt, but he could not understand how to read what they said.

One day, Sparrow flew into the palace through an open window. Now this was a very dangerous thing to do for a little bird. He flew high upon the rafters, looking down until he saw a room filled with books. There were shelves everywhere filled with gilded covers and fancy writing. Sparrow swooped down among the shelves, but the books were too heavy for his tiny beak to open. They were too heavy for him to carry away.

Sparrow started to cry. Mournful little chirps came from his beak. From the corner, perched on a soft window seat, a little princess heard his sobs.

"Little sparrow, why are you crying?" she asked. "Let me open the window. You can fly outside and go home."

But Sparrow wouldn't fly. Instead, he pecked his beak at all the letters. One by one, he pecked and pecked until the little princess asked, with a big smile on her face, "Are you trying to read?"

Little Sparrow nodded his tufted head. The princess took a fairy tale book down from the shelf and slowly read the tiny bird a story. Sparrow sat mesmerized, trying to remember each and every sound the letters made.

Soon, darkness was setting, and the princess had to leave the library. "Fly into the rafters, little sparrow, and sleep. Tomorrow morning, I will bring you some bread and water, and we will read another fairy tale together." Little Sparrow's heart was bursting with such happiness that he barely slept a wink.

That night, the willow tree was so quiet that all the other creatures thought something terrible had happened to Sparrow. They heard no songs, no messages; the forest was very still. Not one chirp of gossip came from willow's branches and tiny Sparrow's beak.

The next morning, the princess came with bread and food and tiny seed cakes for the bird. "Which story shall we read next?" she asked. Little Sparrow pecked at the pages until his beak came across a picture of a beautiful bird. "I guess you want to hear that one," laughed the princess. And she read little Sparrow the story.

This arrangement continued the next morning, and the next, and the mornings after that. Little Sparrow watched very closely and began recognizing little words. Soon, he was reading short sentences. After that, he was reading along with the princess.

Such wonderful tales! Such worlds and adventures and beings unlike any he had ever seen! But little sparrows need more than books. Soon, he began to miss the willow, miss his friends, and miss the wind on his feathers as he flew through the sky.

Little Sparrow chewed his tiny piece of seed cake into very small crumbs. He arranged the crumbs into the words "GOOD BYE" on the bookshelf. Then, his little beak plucked a soft feather out of his chest and laid it upon his favorite fairy tale book. He would never forget the letters and words and stories. Most of all, he would never forget the love his heart carried for a little princess. But he had stories to tell, he had pamphlets to read, and he had signs to explore. And he had

many friends who were waiting to listen.

Wishing on a Star

Once upon a time, in the dead of winter, a little mouse was born. He was snug in his nest deep under the snow, cozy and warm. Mama had stored up seeds, nuts, and acorns for the long winter months.

"When spring comes, we will go outside," she whispered. "It is beautiful in the sunshine, but even more beautiful at night. There are hundreds and hundreds of stars in the sky, my son. And you can make a wish on one. Our nest is under the North Star, the brightest twinkle in the sky."

Baby mouse tried to imagine a star. He could only peek through a very tiny opening and smell the cold air. How he wanted to see the stars!

One night, while mama was fast asleep, baby mouse crept outside. He was very cold, colder than he had ever been. He wished he had mama's furry tummy to snuggle against. Up in the sky, baby mouse saw a large, yellow light shining brightly. Around the light, he saw hundreds and hundreds of twinkling lights. *These are the stars*, baby mouse thought. *They are so beautiful. I must think of my wish.*

But baby mouse was not used to the night and the dangers that lurked. Suddenly, two very bright stars glowed in the nearby bushes. *Are these stars too?* he thought. But the eyes moved, and a black shadow came towards him. Baby mouse felt fear; he raced as fast as he could and hid under the trees.

Now baby mouse was lost. He did not know from which direction he ran, only that he was quite far from the tiny nest opening where mama slept. How was he going to get home? Baby mouse began to cry. "I know my wish," he squeaked. "I want to go home."

The night was scary. The stars became blurred through baby mouse's tears. All at once, he heard a tiny rustling in the dry, winter leaves. A tiny mole twitched his whiskers.

"Who are you? I cannot see very well, but I can smell you. You smell like a mouse. Why are you out on this winter's night?" the mole asked.

"I am lost. I wanted to see the stars, but now I just want to go home. Do you know where my mama's nest is?"

The mole thought for a moment, then spoke. "I know all the underground tunnels around here, but I don't know which one is hers. Do you know anything else about its location?"

Baby mouse tried to remember everything mama had taught him. Everything about the night, the stars, and the world outside raced through his thoughts. "Mama told me about the brightest star in the sky, the North Star. She said it was above our nest."

"Hmmmmm," answered the mole. "The North Star. I don't know which one that is. But I know someone who does."

So baby mouse climbed onto the mole's furry back. His back was furry like mama's, but not as nice. It was stinky and smelly and caked with dirt. Together, they crept through the leaves and twigs until they came to a hollow in the tree.

"Whooooooo goes there?" came a deep voice.

Baby mouse shuddered. Mole said not to be afraid. It was Mr. Owl, the wisest being in the forest. Mr. Owl was a kind owl; he never chased moles or mice. Instead, he ate seeds and nuts and fruits, for he was a very wise owl indeed. "He will know the North Star," Mole whispered.

Mole and baby mouse asked the owl if he knew about the North Star. "Why, yes," hooted Mr. Owl. "The North Star guides all who are lost home. When you find the star, you find your way."

"Please, Mr. Owl, show me the star," baby mouse cried.

Mr. Owl raised his feathered wing and pointed to the brightest twinkle in the sky. "There she is."

Baby mouse looked up in the sky. Now he knew the way home!

"I wish, I wish, upon this star

Please lead me home to mama

For her nest is very far."

The North Star's gleam shone down upon a tiny hole in the ground. Baby mouse sniffed the air. It seemed familiar. He was home!

"Good bye, Mole. Thank you for helping me. When I am older, I will visit with you again." With that, baby mouse scampered through the hole. Mama was still sleeping.

Baby mouse snuggled next to her warm, furry tummy and dreamed of the brightest star in the night sky. One day, he would tell mama about his adventures. But not tonight. With a yawn, he fell asleep.

Mouse grew to be a very wise being, for he knew the North Star. He would help many hungry friends find food in the forest. With him as a guide, they always found their way home again. He lived the remainder of his life in his nest under the North Star, and when he took his final breath, his body lay in peace under her constant, welcoming beams.

The Fairy and the Ghost

Once upon a time, there lived a little fairy. She was quite beautiful and tiny as a thimble. No one could see her. She wandered among the flowers and the ivy and was very, very sad.

How she wished for a friend! She wished for someone to laugh with, to share honey teacakes and hibiscus tea with at lunch, and to wish good night to under the moon and stars.

Sometimes, she tried to fly by the faces of humans, but they just swatted her away like a pesky fly. Sometimes, she tried to make friends with the birds and squirrels, but they just scratched at her like a tiny flea. She was very sad and alone.

One day, the little fairy saw a shimmering orb in the sky. It was very tiny, but just the right size for a fairy's eyes. The orb swirled and glistened a rainbow of colors in the sunlight. The fairy thought it was very beautiful. She spread her tiny fairy wings and flew beside it.

"Can you see me?" cried the orb.

"Yes," said the fairy, "I can see you. What is your name?"

"My name is Charlotte. I am a ghost. Humans don't believe in me, and most don't see me. Some do see me and think I am just a speck of dust and swat their hands at me. I am so lonely. Who are you?" the little orb asked.

"My name is Daffodil," answered the fairy. "I am lonely too. No one believes in me, either. They swat at me and think I am a bug. But all I want is a friend. I have wished for a friend to laugh with, a friend to share tea with, and a friend to tell good night to under the moon and stars. Will you be my friend, Charlotte?" the fairy asked.

Suddenly, a face appeared inside the little orb. It was the face of a tiny girl with a warm smile and tear-filled eyes. "Yes, I will be your friend, Daffodil. We will fly through the flowers and laugh among the trees and collect dew drops for afternoon tea."

"What is a ghost?" asked Daffodil.

"A ghost is a human who does not have a body any longer but has a heart and soul," answered Charlotte. "What is a fairy?" Charlotte asked.

"A fairy is a being that has a heart and soul and fairy wings and magick," Daffodil replied.

Together, Charlotte and Daffodil danced among the heather, slept inside the downy tufts of thistles under the moon, and made wishes on the dandelion seeds. But there weren't many wishes left to make. Daffodil's and Charlotte's wishes had already come true. They were best friends forever.

The Opossum Will See You Now

Beatrice was an opossum. Her friends called her Bea. She lived in a forest that grew adjacent to a tiny, rural village. Everyone loved Bea. She was so kind, always willing to lend a hand or help a friend in need.

In this village was a country veterinarian. He tended cats, dogs, cows, and horses. He was loved as much as Bea was for his kindness towards all.

Bea wanted to be a vet. She saw the dogs and cats go into Dr. Miles' office and walk out, tails wagging and noses sniffing the air. So many woodland friends needed help. So many were injured and sick and did not have a place to go or a doctor to see.

You may know that opossums are very quiet and curl up into tiny balls. Bea entered the attic rafter of Dr. Miles' office each early morning before sunrise and spent her day curled up, listening to all his treatments and advice. She wanted to learn how to help all the others. Right now, Charlie Chipmunk had a painful tooth, Timmy Rabbit had an earache, and Mrs. Fox was due to give birth any day. There was so much to learn, so much to listen to, so much to see. Bea watched each day from the dusty rafter in the ceiling.

It was springtime; the trees and flowers were blooming. But that was not a good thing for Bea. She sneezed in the spring. The dusty rafter wasn't helping her opossum nose's sneezing either. Bea learned other animals reacted the same way in springtime. Many came in to see Dr. Miles, and they were sneezing too.

Dr. Miles had just finished up his last appointment when he heard a loud *ACHOO*.......

"Who's there?" asked Dr. Miles.

Bea was very frightened. She didn't know what to do. Should she run? Just then, another loud *ACHOO*......

Dr. Miles looked up and saw opossum eyes peering down from the ceiling rafter.

"Hello, Dr. Miles. I think I need an antihistamine. These spring allergies are making me sneeze."

"You certainly know a lot about medicine," Dr. Miles exclaimed. "How did you become so smart?"

"From watching you every day," Bea answered.

"You mean to tell me you have sat here every day?" Dr. Miles could hardly believe it. Bea told Dr. Miles about her friends. She told him how they needed care. She told him about Charlie, about Timmy, and about Mrs. Fox.

"Well, we cannot have you sneezing in the rafters any longer," said Dr. Miles. "Tomorrow morning, eight o'clock sharp, be here at my office. Bring this medicine to Mrs. Fox, and tell her it will help with her pain. And take this medicine for your sneezing."

Bea tucked the medicine in her pouch and scurried off to the woods. How excited she was. She was going to learn to be a vet!

Each morning, Bea came at eight o'clock sharp. She assisted Dr. Miles and learned about bandaging and diagnosing all sorts of ailments.

Dr. Miles got out a huge encyclopedia of healing herbs and taught Bea about the natural remedies of the woodlands. She learned which bark helped pain, which roots to boil for teas, and which plants could cause illness and allergies. Bea would wander the woodlands in the early evenings, search for these natural remedies, and store them in her pouch.

Soon, Bea was expecting a family of her own. Along with her herbs and teas, her babies piled on board inside her pouch. They learned which plants to pick, which seeds to eat, and how to brew teas and make tinctures.

When her babies grew old enough, they scampered to neighboring villages and all became healing opossums as well. Animals came from all over the woodlands to seek their help. No longer need they suffer with toothaches, stomachaches, and ailing bones.

Dr. Miles' kindness helped all the animals in his village, and his kindness towards a little opossum helped countless others for miles around. Before he retired, Dr. Miles gave Bea a little wooden sign. She hung it outside her little tree hollow home. It read,

The opossum will see you now.
Office of Beatrice, Woodland Vet

No matter what hour of the day or night, Bea was always ready to help an animal in need. Her tree became a healing sanctuary in the woodlands.

Running Away

Once upon a time, a little boy set off on an early autumn day. He held a burlap sack with a slice of bread, an apple, and a tiny jar of honey. In his arms, he cradled a fuzzy stuffed horse that his mother had sewn for him. He had planned this adventure for a long time—since early morning, when his mother had sent him to his room as punishment. He would run away to a place where little boys could misbehave and eat only sweets for dinner and never have to listen to anyone.

It was late afternoon now. The boy knew his mother would be setting their table for dinner. His little tummy was surely hungry, but he had places to go. So he took his slice of bread out of his sack and took a bite. Down swooped a tiny robin.

"Might I have a bite?" the robin chirped. "I am so hungry. I have been flying since early morning, for it is autumn and the snows will soon be here. I haven't found a worm in days. Why are you journeying? Are you looking for food, too?" he asked the boy.

"No," said the boy, "my mother always fills my plate."

"Are you looking for shelter from the snow?" chirped the robin.

"No, my bed is soft and warm, with many blankets to cover me."

The robin shook his head, but happily accepted the crumbs of bread and journeyed on. The boy took out his apple and took a bite.

Soon, the boy came upon a bear. He was a tiny bear, and this was his first autumn on his own. "Please, little boy, may I have a bite of your apple? I have to eat as much as I can before I go to sleep, before the winter snow comes. No more fruit is on the trees, and no more berries grace the bushes. You are so lucky to have a delicious apple," he sighed. "Why are you journeying so late on this path all by yourself? Are you looking for fruit and berries, too?"

"No," said the boy. "My mother jars apples and peaches and berries from the garden. We have them all winter long."

The bear shook his head quizzically and took a bite of apple. Then he journeyed on.

All the boy had left at this point was a bit of crust and honey. He dipped the crust into the jar and took a bite. Soon, a tiny butterfly flitted to his shoulder. "Oh, please, may I have a drop of honey?" the butterfly asked. "I am so weary, and I have hundreds and hundreds of miles to go before I reach my home. Why are *you* journeying?"

"Because I did not listen to my mother," the boy said. "She made me go to my room."

"How I wish I had my own room for the winter!" sighed the butterfly. "Do you know I have to share my tree with thousands of other butterflies?"

"Thousands!" cried the boy.

"Yes," squeaked the butterfly as she dipped her mouth into the sweet nectar. Then, she spread her wings and let the wind carry her off.

The day's light soon faded, and the little boy's legs grew very tired. How he wished for all the good food at his mother's table. How he longed for his soft, warm bed. His comfy room didn't seem like punishment now. In fact, it seemed like paradise.

By now, the little boy was horribly lost. The sun had set, and the wind sent a chill down his tiny legs. Too tired to go on any further, he closed his eyes and fell asleep, his tiny, sewn horse nestled in his arms. He dreamed of his mother's apples and peaches, he dreamed of bread drenched in honey, and he dreamed of soft pillows and warm blankets.

A tiny fairy came upon the sleeping boy. Little fairies come out in the darkness. When all the people and all the animals are fast asleep, the fairies begin their day. This tiny fairy landed on the little boy's nose until he twitched and opened his eyes.

"Why are you out in the woods so late at night?" she asked the boy.

"I wanted to run away, but now all I wish is to go home," he cried.

The fairy was looking at the tiny, stuffed horse cradled in the little boy's arms. "If I take you home, will you give me your horse?" asked the fairy.

The little boy loved this horse. He slept with him every night, and he carried him around every day. But the little boy wanted to go home to his mother, to his room, to his bed. Reluctantly, he said yes.

He placed the little horse by the fairy's feet. His toy was bigger than she was. All of a sudden, the little fairy touched the horse's mane and he became *real!*

"Thank you, little boy. I have seen humans ride horses and always longed to have one of my own. You have made my wish come true." The tiny fairy climbed on top of the miniature horse. She motioned for the little boy to follow as she led him on the path to home. As they neared his cottage, the boy saw many lights in the woods. Many villagers were searching for him.

"Farewell," said the fairy. "I must leave you now. Go home." With that, she galloped away as fast as lightning, the tiny horse's legs prancing in the moonlight.

The boy was so tired, he scarcely remembered being placed in his bed. As his head sunk down onto his soft pillow, he felt the fuzzy mane of his beloved stuffed horse. From his windowsill, a tiny fairy smiled and waved goodbye.

Diamond in the Moon

In a little park, there lived a mated pair of sparrows. A willow tree held their nest, so finely crafted of twigs and bark and dried grass. Each day, visitors to the park left treasures for the little male sparrow. Tiny pieces of foil gum wrappers, little girls' hair ribbons, a lost glove dropped to the ground. Each forgotten and lost piece was a treasure, gently woven into a masterpiece for his beloved.

One day, the little sparrow spotted something gleaming in the sunlight. It was a beautiful ring. "Oh," he sighed. "What a beautiful gift for my mate." The sparrow opened his beak and picked up the ring. He flew up to the willow and dropped it at her feet. His mate had never seen something so beautiful! It shone in the sun more vividly than any gum wrapper. It was the most beautiful present in the whole world!

Skillfully, the male sparrow wove pieces of grass around the ring, securing it in place. He puffed out his little sparrow chest in pride at his find. That night, the little ring's diamond glistened in the moonlight. It was a tiny night light in their nest, and the little sparrows loved it so.

The following morning, the tiny male sparrow was out looking for seeds when he noticed a pair of visitors to the park. The male was looking everywhere; in fact, he reminded sparrow of himself. *Perhaps he is building a nest too*, the sparrow thought. The female was chirping softly, tears falling down her face. Little sparrow could see she was very unhappy. Quietly, he watched and listened.

"We shall never find it," she cried. "It is lost forever." Her mate tried his best to comfort her, but little sparrow could see it was fruitless. Then, the keen eyes of the little sparrow saw the male's mate hold up her fingers to the sun. "It is gone forever; no longer will I see it sparkle in the sun!"

Just then, little sparrow's heart sank deep within his chest. For he knew why she cried, and he knew what he must do. He flew to the nest and told his mate. Carefully, he chewed the bits of grass that held their treasure. He placed it in his beak and flew down to the visitors' feet. His beloved watched with sorrowful eyes.

The searching pair didn't notice him at first, but then the female saw him and saw what he held in his beak. "My ring!!!!!!" she cried. The little sparrow dropped his treasure and nodded his tiny head to her. "Thank you, little sparrow," they cried. They watched him fly back to the willow tree, back to his nest and to his beloved mate.

So grateful to the little sparrow, the pair returned to the park each spring. They brought seeds and soft pieces of yarn and sparkling pieces of tissue paper with glitter that gleamed in the sun. The male put penny after penny in

• • •

gumball machines until he finally won a huge *diamond* ring. The spring that he left it was the best spring of little sparrow's life. His mate's eyes sparkled almost as brightly when he gave it to her.

"This one is yours to keep," he chirped. He wove it inside their nest, and each night, the moon captured its sparkle like a star.

The visitors never stopped being grateful to the tiny birds. The human male gave his mate a beautiful pair of crystal sparrows for their wedding anniversary. They returned for several years, but alas, the number of springs for tiny birds is far fewer than for people. The spring came when the couple returned to the willow to find the nest empty.

The male reached high into the branches and gently lifted the nest from its perch. He had never seen how truly beautiful it was. He could recognize faded bits of yarn and paper. Then, he saw it. The gumball machine ring, carefully woven inside.

The couple took the nest home and placed it on their windowsill. Within it sat the beautiful pair of crystal sparrows the male had given his beloved some springs ago. At night, the moonlight shimmered on the pair, and in the sunlight, the gumball ring created rainbows throughout the room.

Treasured

In a village many centuries ago lived a handsome and rich highwayman. He preyed upon innocent travelers, robbing them of their money and jewels. He possessed all the material gifts that life could bring, but he possessed little else. He had no friends; he trusted no one.

The years were unkind to this highwayman. His good looks vanished, his bones grew twisted with arthritis, and his eyes no longer sparkled like the jewels he had buried so long ago. He now spent his days wandering, unable to journey back to the place where his treasures were hidden. Soon, he became totally blind, begging for pieces of bread. No one helped him except a kind monk who traveled past him on the road one day. To all others, he became invisible—or a leper to be untouched.

The village dogs who wandered the roads did not see him as a leper; instead, they saw him as a man. They would nuzzle his scraggly beard, lick his bruised feet, and guide him to the village dumps for leftover scraps of nourishment. For the first time in his life, the beggar man knew what it was like to trust, knew what it was like to love.

His shallow heart grew very deep, and he felt sorrow for all the wrong he had done in his life. But it was too late. *I am dying now*, he thought. *It is too late for me to undo the sorrow I caused in my youth.*

The old man lay down by the side of the road. The dogs tugged at his ragged clothes, but he told them to go on ahead. He was so tired; his days of wandering were over.

Then, an Angel appeared before him. He could see her, even though his eyes had not seen even a shadow for so long. How beautiful she was! She smiled upon him and asked him if he were truly sorry for his unkind ways. The old man nodded.

"Then you shall do penance here on earth for a time," she whispered. With a bright flash of light, the Angel disappeared.

The old beggar awoke, thinking it was a very strange dream. But he could see now! And when he looked down upon his body, he saw that his was now different, one with fur and paws and a tail!

Villagers were traveling the road but did not see him. He wandered into town, but no one knew he was there! *Oh,* he thought, forgetting for one moment the kind ways and remembering his life of sin. *What treasures I can steal! Why, I can walk right into the king's palace and take anything I desire!*

Thankfully, though, the man soon realized that he needed no treasures. Truth be told, he wasn't even hungry now. Strange, he had been hungry for years and years, but now no food tempted his sharp eyes.

Then, he heard a little child's cries. He moved in its direction and saw a lost toddler, huddled in an alley. The angel dog lay down by her side, licking her tears and soothing her fears. She stroked his fur, which was a touch of kindness he felt deep within his heart. The child's parents came and swept her in their arms. She told them of the kind dog, but they thought she was imagining him and quickly walked toward home.

The angel dog began wandering the village, looking for all the forlorn and forgotten people. Those who were untouched, unloved. Only they could see him; only they could pet his soft coat of fur; only they could hold his paws in their gnarled and wrinkled fingers.

Much time passed, although the angel dog knew little of the passage of time anymore. He needed no sleep; his nights were spent walking the darkened roadways, aiding those who were lost, those who had been beaten and robbed, those who had been cheated by men—the kind like he used to be.

One night, the beautiful Angel reappeared. "You have done well," she said as she smiled at the large dog. "Now, I will give you one final choice. You may come back and join the living here in this world again. You may come back as the handsome man of your youth, or you may rejoin the living as a large dog. If you return as a dog, you must remember your time on earth will be much shorter, for a dog's time is much less than a man's."

The angel dog thought for a moment. In his entire life, the only kindness he had ever felt was from a village monk and from the village strays. The treasures of jewels and money held no allure to his eyes any longer. His heart had never felt such fullness as when he licked a crying child's face or nuzzled the cheek of a weary leper.

"I shall remain a dog."

With that, the Angel again vanished within a glowing light. The dazed man looked upon his surroundings. He felt the same. His eyes were sharp. His fur was soft. His large paws felt the ground. But he was hungry!

Then, he remembered. He remembered where he had buried his jewels and money. The dog ran through the woods, through the trees, his heart beating wildly. He reached the spot and furiously pawed at the dirt. He uncovered the satchel. He grasped it in his teeth and ran back to the village. He came upon a large, wooden door. This was the place. He started barking and barking. It was nighttime, and every occupant was asleep except one.

A monk opened the door. His kind, familiar face looked upon the dog. "Are you hungry, my friend? I will get you something to eat." Then, the monk saw the satchel. "What is this?" he asked.

The monk opened the bag of jewels and money, his amazed mouth gaping wide. He had seen such jewels before; his own family had been very wealthy. But the monk had given all this up to serve a humble life of faith and kindness. The monk knelt down in prayer, thanking the Lord for this gift. What it could do to help the poor and the sick! It would even help build the new village church. He took the satchel and gestured for the large dog to come inside.

For many years, the monk and the large dog wandered the roads, helping those who were untouched, unseen, and unloved. Others called the monk Francis. The dog just called him friend.

The Milkweed and the Monarch

In a country farmer's sunny field, a beautiful milkweed grew. She grew tall and straight, with many blossoms and big, green seed pouches to provide shelter for her sleeping babies. She was one of the last of her kind; her brothers and sisters had all been cut down or sprayed with chemicals that made them very sick. Most people didn't like milkweed in their gardens. Most didn't understand the gentleness of these nurturing plants.

There she stood, quite lonely in the midday sun. Then along came a little grasshopper. "Hmmm," said the grasshopper. "Your big, green leaves look mighty tasty. I think I'll try a bite." He started to munch. "Yuck!!!" he screamed. "These taste awful."

Milkweed smiled and waved her leaf in a farewell gesture as the grasshopper hopped away.

Then along came a praying mantis. "Hmmm, my belly is growling. These leaves will be my lunch." He took a bite. "Phewy!!!" he yelled. "These leaves are disgusting!"

Milkweed just laughed and bowed her long, tall stem to praying mantis as he leaped away.

Soon came a beautiful butterfly. She was orange and black with beautiful spots on her wings. "Hello, Mrs. Milkweed," the butterfly squeaked. "I have been searching for you." With that, the tiny butterfly closed her delicate wings and nestled on a leaf. "I am a monarch, and your leaves are the only place on which I can lay my eggs. Please take care of them for me, for I must fly away to far off lands."

Mother Milkweed protected the tiny eggs from the winds and rains of summer. She curled her leaves to hide them when other hungry bugs flew by. Summer days began to fade and soon the little eggs hatched into tiny babies. The babies didn't look like the beautiful orange and black butterfly, though.

One of the babies opened her tiny eyes and looked up at Mrs. Milkweed's lovely green leaf. "I am so hungry," the baby squeaked and began munching away at her leaves.

Mrs. Milkweed loved the little babies. They were striped and squiggly, with fuzzy legs and little antennae on top of their heads. The little babies loved Mrs. Milkweed, too. Without her, they would starve. With Mrs. Milkweed's nourishing leaves, they grew big and strong.

Mrs. Milkweed's own babies were growing, too. Her seedpods were changing color and opening, and her little seeds began blowing in the wind. As each one departed, Mrs. Milkweed bid them a tearful goodbye. "Find a sunny field to sleep upon, my children," she cried. She watched the wind carry them up to the skies.

Soon, the monarch's babies were leaving as well. "Good bye, Mrs. Milkweed," they squeaked. "We must find a tree and go to sleep also. Thank you for taking such good care of us." Mrs. Milkweed watched each one squiggle away. Now, just a few of her seedpods were left. Soon, she would follow suit and go to sleep within the ground.

Days passed. The summer nights grew cooler, and the blossoms began to droop. Autumn was soon approaching. Mrs. Milkweed tried to stand as tall as before, but her stem grew weary and wilted in the afternoon sun. The last of her baby seeds were left, clinging to her pods, fearful of journeying alone in the sky.

Suddenly, a little orange and black butterfly landed on her seedpod. "Hello, Mother Milkweed," she said. "I am one of your butterfly babies. I have come to say goodbye. I must go on a very long journey. It is a journey high into the sky, into the winds and rain, to a distant place where I can rest for the winter. I came to kiss you goodbye."

Mother Milkweed started to cry, tears rolling down her stem. The little seeds told her not to cry. "Don't cry, mama. We won't leave you," they whispered.

"You must leave me, my children. If you don't, you will not see the next summer sun and become tall milkweed plants yourselves."

"Don't be afraid," said the little monarch. "Come with me. I will carry you."

The little seeds clung tightly to the monarch's fuzzy body. They were light as air; the monarch hardly felt them. With one last flutter of her wings, the monarch gently kissed Mother Milkweed goodbye. The little seeds all fluttered their fluff and waved goodbye. Off they went.

The monarch soared high into the sky. She soared through the clouds. She flew with the stars and moon. She flew with the rain and thunder and lightning, all the while shielding the tiny seeds as she traveled. As they passed over peaceful country fields, the monarch let each of them go and watched them flutter to the ground. "Rest now. One day, I will find you again, and you will help my children grow."

All but one seed left. She was very frightened and clung so tightly that the little monarch could not let her go. On and on they traveled, over large rivers and beside flocks of migrating birds. Finally, they came to a beautiful forest of tall trees. Thousands and thousands of butterflies slept in the trees.

"Little seed, I must go to sleep now. I will gently place you on the ground. Go to sleep, too. Don't be afraid. I promise you will be all right."

With that, the tired, little seed dropped to the soft earth and burrowed in the ground. Within a moment, she was fast asleep. The little monarch was so tired too. She gently fluttered her wings back and forth for a few moments and then drifted off to peaceful slumber.

All winter they slept. Then, one warm, sunny morning, the little monarch lifted her head. Her antennae felt the warm breeze, the breeze that summoned her home on another long journey. She opened her wings and heard a quiet squeak from the ground.

A tiny stem sprouted in the earth below. "I will wait for you," the little seed sighed and furled her tiny leaves around a short but very straight stem.

Basil's England

Basil Ratbone was a distinguished rat from a very distinguished family. He could trace his lineage all the way back to England, though now he lived in a large hotel in New York City. Basil's great, great, great, great, great, great, great, great, great, great-grandmother once lived at Chawton, Jane Austen's house in Hampshire, England. (Rats have a lot of great-grandmothers you know, so from this point onward, I will just refer to Basil's ancestral grandmother as great-grandma.)

Basil's own grandmother told him stories of Jane reading in the family's big room, which was filled with books of many subjects. Basil's great-grandma learned to read there, late at night, when all the family was asleep. She taught all her children to read. They, in turn, taught all their children, and so Basil himself had the gift of knowing what words meant.

Basil's relatives had slipped on board a great ship and sailed across the ocean to America centuries ago. They made a new home in New York City, but they always spoke of the peace and green of England and the wonderful teas and crumpet and scone crumbs left for them to enjoy.

Basil had many friends in the hotel. There were families of mice and spiders to visit him in his private basement nook. There were also hundreds of roaches, but Basil didn't like to fraternize with them. He found their habits too untidy and beneath his standards of propriety.

Basil held tea each afternoon. It was formal dress. Mrs. Mouse always wore her best lace collar and woolen skirt. The spiders wove delicate lace tablecloths for Basil's small table. A porcelain doll's teacup set from the hotel gift shop served fragrant herbal and floral teas (for which Basil's fellow rat friends searched the hotel gardens each dewy morning before the guests awoke). Each morning, Basil put pebbles out in the hot sun to use as pressing stones for his trousers. He made the creases sharp and crisp. He collected rainwater to wash his woolen shirts, which Mrs. Mouse had so kindly felted for him.

But Basil was not happy. He longed to see England. He wanted to see Jane Austen's house, visit the big room filled with books, and find the rest of his family still remaining there.

In the meantime, Basil liked to learn about the hotel guests, where they came from, where they were going. One day, he heard a man carrying a large suitcase say he had just flown in from London.

"London!" Basil shrieked. "That is in England." He watched and listened as the hotel clerk asked how long he would be staying.

"I have a flight back home in three days," the man replied.

Basil's tiny rat heart was pounding in his chest. *This is my chance*, he thought. *I shall stow away and go back home to England.*

Basil told his friends of his plan. Mrs. Mouse was a worrier; she told him not to go. "It is too dangerous, Basil," she squeaked. But she knew she could not dissuade her friend. She stayed up two nights in a row to felt him the most distinguished vest for his journey. The spiders wove a netted satchel for Basil to put some food and his favorite porcelain teacup inside. The netting was strong so Basil's cup would not break during the long journey.

Three days later, Basil crept to the Englishman's room and slid under the door. He found the man still asleep. Basil tiptoed to the large suitcase and crawled inside a pocket. It was warm and dark and smelled of strange smells. *Maybe this is what England smells like,* Basil thought. Soon, he fell asleep.

Basil awoke to the jostle and bumping of someone banging his suitcase along the floor. Soon, he was riding in the hotel elevator. Next, he was loaded into the smelly trunk of a cab. "Phew!" Basil shrieked. "This isn't England!"

The ride was long and bumpy. Basil had a headache by the time they stopped. When the trunk opened, Basil peeked out and squinted his tiny rodent eyes in the bright sun. He had never seen this place before. Lots and lots of people, all carrying big suitcases, were walking very fast around him. *They must all be going to England,* he thought.

Basil quickly ducked down into the pocket again and waited. The Englishman picked up his suitcase and carried it inside. Basil very gingerly lifted his head, only enough so that his two rat eyes could see what was happening.

"Oh no!" he exclaimed. He saw men and women opening suitcases and checking inside. "What if they find me!" he cried.

Basil saw the suitcases moving along a big machine and going into a back room. *They are on their way to England*, he thought. Basil knew what he must do. He summoned all his rat courage and jumped from the pocket. A woman screamed! He was spotted.

Basil ran like the wind. He ran toward the back room where the suitcases were going. He ran between people's legs, he hid among large purses and tote bags, and finally, he made it! He was in the back room. Basil's heart was racing, and he was very tired. He crawled inside another suitcase pocket, this one smelling like perfume. Basil liked that. Soon, he was being tossed and jostled again, much harder than before. But Basil didn't mind. He was so exhausted, he slept through it all.

When he awoke, he was in a dark, cold place. He snuggled inside the suitcase pocket and ate the tiny cake Mrs. Mouse had packed for him. How he longed for some hot tea. How he missed his lace tablecloth, his porcelain teapot, his friends. For the first time, Basil started to cry.

Then, he thought of England. He thought of the big room filled with books, the afternoon teas, and his family still at Chawton. Basil took out the nice felt handkerchief Mrs. Mouse made for him and wiped his tears.

Basil heard the sound of large machines, much louder than the hotel's furnace that woke him in the basement. Soon the noise was quiet, and Basil felt the jostling and bumping again. He moved through a room (similar to the one he had escaped to) and saw a lot of people, all carrying suitcases and hurriedly walking like before in New York City.

But this wasn't New York City. He heard a woman's voice call out the words, "Heathrow Airport." *Heathrow! I am in England. I am home,* Basil thought to himself.

Through a tiny tear in the suitcase pocket, Basil saw a pretty woman reach for her bag. She lifted it and got into a waiting car. Basil stayed very, very still and quiet, barely breathing; he didn't want to frighten her. He didn't understand why, but most people were frightened of him and started screaming whenever he was near. They arrived at a large train station. Basil had read about trains from a pamphlet left by a hotel guest. "Now to find Chawton," he whispered to himself.

Basil crept down from the pocket when no one was watching. He slid down into a dark corner of the tracks and rested for a moment. Soon, a very large rat appeared.

"Who are you?" he asked.

"I am Basil. I am looking for Chawton. Can you help me get there?"

"Sure, I know all the places around England," the rat boasted. "Why are you dressed so fancy? Don't you know people hate us. Me and my buddies don't dress up anymore. We hunt around for scraps and never take baths."

Basil was very sad to hear this. Maybe England wasn't the same anymore. Maybe there was no place for distinguished rats. Maybe there were no afternoon teas, no scones and crumpets, no lace tablecloths.

"C'mon," said the large rat. "I will show you the train to Chawton. No rat that looks like you would last a day around here." With that, he motioned Basil to hurry on and follow.

"Keep your head down and out of sight!" the big rat advised. "Don't let anybody see you! Say 'hi' to your distinguished rats in Chawton. Tell them Sherlock told you the way." With a whisk of his tail, Sherlock was gone, disappearing down the tracks.

Basil did as he was told. He hid on the train, barely breathing. The ride was long, but Basil could not rest. He kept sniffing the air, waiting to sniff the tea, the crumpets, and the scones of his great-grandma's home.

When the train stopped, Basil listened to the guides giving directions. "That way to Jane Austen's house," one of them remarked.

Basil set forth. He walked for many hours, for a tiny rat's feet take tiny rat steps. He wandered among the beautiful green his grandmother had told him about. He sniffed the flowers in the air that made the beautiful teas. Finally, a beautiful brick home towered above him. Basil crept inside through a tiny crack in the basement.

There, seated in a nook, were several rats, a family of mice, and some spiders. There was a delicate lace tablecloth on the table. Porcelain teacups and a fine teapot graced the lace doilies, and tempting crumbs of scones and crumpets invited hungry mouths.

"Who are you?" a kind, white whiskered rat asked.

"I am Basil Ratbone," Basil proudly answered. Basil reached into his spider web satchel and lifted out a porcelain teacup. It was a perfect match to the set adorning the lace tablecloth before him.

"Ratbone!" the motherly rat replied. "Why, you are my great, great, great, great, great, great, great, great, great,

great......Well, you know, grandson." Motherly grandma rats have a lot of grandsons. "Come join us, Basil," she squeaked. "We have been waiting for one of you to return."

Basil was home. He took a deep rat breath and sniffed the air. This was England. This was home. He hoped no one noticed the tiny rat tear that fell from his eye.

Tinged with Grey

Nothing tugs my heartstrings harder

And I can truly say

That no face is quite so lovely

As a face that's tinged

With grey

No youthful, glossy muzzle

No sprightly, springy prance

Can make my heart yearn half so

As the years of final dance

Years of loving, gentle friendship

When the puppy days are past

Win my heart, paws down, each moment

From my first sight

Until my last..........

My House

My childhood home

Still standing

Although just a frame of wood

For just a shadow lingers

Where a house in sunshine stood

My home now stands

In memories

Though walls and floors remain

My memories hold the contents

Of laughter and of pain

The garden path still lingers

Though the rose arbor is lost

The tiger lilies missing

As in perpetual frost

My parents now dwell elsewhere

In a distant Realm and time

Now all that's left

Is peeling paint

From a house

Once in her prime

Once roses graced the pathway

Where a child's initials lay

In freshly mixed concrete

To mark that memory day

My daddy said

Those letters

Would last longer than he

And all who came to read them

This memory would see

Of a father and his daughter

A tiny stick in hand

Who traced SAR in a mixture

Of water, rocks, and sand

Water lasts forever

Rising, falling from the sky

But houses soon are empty

For all within will die

Among the roses of heaven

Among the lilies fair

My house still stands

In sunshine

Waiting for me there.

The Old Woman's Garden

Once there lived a very kind, old woman. Her hair was white and her eyes were crinkled, but still they sparkled as she greeted all the animals who came to her door each day.

The birds came from the sky. The moles burrowed from out of the earth. The squirrels climbed down from the trees. The little ducks raised their heads from the pond. All creatures were greeted each day by her open hands as they tossed crumbs of bread or bits of grain and pieces of apples to their hungry mouths. The old woman had a beautiful garden with tall oaks, lavender, and dandelion blossoms. The old woman loved dandelions. She never pulled them up, but rather cherished the tiny puffs that flew on the breeze. All were welcome to share in this garden—the rabbits, the chipmunks, and the birds all found seeds and shelter there.

The woman kept to herself. Her friends were the creatures of the forest. Her secrets were shared with them, her tears were cried to them, her songs were sung to only them. Other villagers would come by, selling eggs, flour, and handmade goods. The woman greeted them kindly, but her heart remained always shielded from human touch. Much heartache as a child had brought her to the animals, to the kindness of those often treated cruelly by man.

Colonies of cats would wander to her door. Of course, they looked for food. But more than that, they looked for the woman's kindness and friendship. They trusted her to wrap their injured paws, wash their reddened eyes, rub healing balm on their itchy skin. Feral dogs tracked to her door as well. They chose her barn to have their puppies in safety (since this was a world where little ones often faced dangers).

The old woman lived a long, long life. Her back was bent, but her crinkled eyes never lost their luster until her final days. No longer did she go outside to greet her family. They still came. The birds and cats and squirrels. The ducks and geese and foxes and opossums. They all came and waited. But she did not open her door.

Little sparrows flew to her bedroom windowsill and peeked inside. She lay on her bed, her crinkled eyes closed. They flew inside, tiny crumbs in their beaks, and gently pecked at her lips. However, she would not eat their gifts. Mournfully, the woodland beings waited in the woods and watched, hoping each day she would gain the strength to waken.

Days passed. Finally, a neighboring farmer knocked on her door. Not getting an answer, he opened it and went inside, climbing up the stairs to her bedroom. There, he found her.

• • •

The animals watched as he carried her blanket-wrapped body to his cart. The birds watched from the sky, the squirrels watched from the trees, the opossums from their sheltered burrows under the porch, the wild dogs from her barn. None made a peep, for they feared man.

The sparrows flew along the cart, watching where the farmer took their friend. He brought her to an old church and carried her body inside. The creatures waited in the woods beside the church. They saw some villagers go inside. They saw some men carry their friend to the churchyard and place her body to rest, deep within the earth.

Nightfall came. Under the moonlight, the creatures gathered. The sparrows brought rose petals. The squirrels brought acorns. The feral cats brought beautiful dandelion puffs to place on her grave. The wild dogs brought their puppies to show respect, and the opossums carried lavender in their pouches to adorn her grave.

Together, they worked and created the most beautiful wreath of flowers, herbs, and acorns, more beautiful than any had ever seen before. The next morning, when the parish priest walked by the churchyard, he passed the humble woman's grave and marveled at the wreath's most exquisite craftsmanship. *Who could possibly have left this,* he wondered to himself.

From that morning onward, as the months and years passed, her grave was never barren. Beautiful wreaths adorned its place. No one saw who brought them, though some villagers attempted to keep watch. Some said she was a witch, and it was enchantment. Some feared her grave and refused to pass by, telling stories of ghosts and spirits in the night. Only those that dwelled in the woodlands knew. And they would never forget the kindness of one who lived among a world filled with cruelty.

Centuries passed. The stones in the churchyard all crumbled, the ground giving way to weeds and tall grass. The parishioners were all gone. The tiny woodland beings had all perished or been forced to leave their homes as man encroached. But the seeds of acorns grew into oaks, the dandelions blossomed into yellow flowers, and the lavender continued to fragrance the air around one tiny cross that stood tilted in the yard, tilted as an old, kind woman's back.

The Fairy Wedding

Under the twinkling starlight

In a mossy patch of green

A wedding of the fey folk

To human eyes unseen

Took place one moonlit evening

With dancing, mirth, and glee

And nectar from the flowers

Delivered by the bees

Lilies of the Valley

Adorned the fairy's head

And puffs of dainty dandelions

Blew wishes

As she wed

Her handsome fairy prince

Adorned in willow bark

The wedding song

Sung sweetly

By a forest-dwelling lark

The rings were woven flax

Entwined in twists of love
As the elders gave their blessings
From fairy realms above

No mortal foot would trod
Upon this secret place
For its known only to fairies
Not to the human race

But under twinkling starlight
A teeny mound remains
And a lark sometimes will sing there
Her lilting love refrains.

Fairies in the Snow

Where do little fairies hide
When snow is tumbling fast?
On tiny sleighs of bark they ride
To hidden places fast.

They nestle in the hollow trees
They snuggle in fox dens
They burrow down in rabbit holes
Among the hills and glens.

They wriggle into cairns of rock
They sleep in piles of leaves
Bundled in down feathered frock
They climb in cottage eaves.

And sleep until the daffodils
Awake their tired heads
With cheery, yellow-headed smiles
Among the flower beds.

And then they dance
And dance and dance
Among the daffodils

And set out on their merry paths

To heather laden hills.

Crow and Crone

Once upon a time, in a dark and ancient forest, there lived an old crow. The crow had seen many years. He watched as Princes grew into Kings. He watched as tiny saplings aged into towering trees. But now, the years had taken his keen eyesight, taken his swift wings, taken his sharp ears. He seldom flew down from his high tree, except to snatch a few berries or drink of water. Then, he hurried as quickly as his sparsely feathered wings could carry him back home.

One day, an old woman with gnarled fingers curled around a walking stick saw the crow as he bent down to take a sip of water. "What is your name?" she asked.

This startled the crow. Very few humans knew crows possessed the gift of speech. Crows could talk and remember and recognize all those who passed in the forest. But the old crow did not recognize this woman; he had never seen her before.

"My name is Obsidian," he murmured. "You may call me Sid for short, though. Obsidian is a name of one powerful and strong, not like the crow I have become."

"You look very tired," said the old woman. "Much like me. I must rest now, for I am very weary and my old legs cannot carry me much further."

"I am tired, too," said Sid. "My wings grow heavy now. Once, they could soar into the sky above the clouds. Now, they can barely carry me up to the tallest tree branches."

"Come rest by me," the old woman said. So it came to be that a tired crow and an aging crone sat together, sharing a loaf of bread and chunk of cheese from the old woman's basket.

"I have never seen you before," said Sid. "Why do you travel this forest all alone?

"I am not alone," answered the woman, "for I have found a friend to share my meal and keep me company."

The sun was setting. It was time for Sid to perch in his tree for the night. This was going to be a cold night; the wind was bristling through the branches. Within minutes, the old woman had drifted off to sound sleep. Sid did not want to leave the kind woman alone in the forest. He grabbed her shawl in his beak and wrapped it around her as best as he could and perched on top of her walking stick, closing his eyes for the night. No human had ever taken the time to speak with him before. For the first time in his long life, Sid didn't feel so lonely. He soon fell fast asleep.

In the morning, Sid awoke to find the old woman still sleeping. He gently nudged her hand with his beak and said, "Good morning."

"Good morning, Sid," answered the crone. "It is time to continue on my journey. Would you like to come with me?" she asked.

Sid wanted to go, but he knew his wings could not carry him, his legs did not have strength enough to walk, and his eyes and ears were not keen enough to protect him any longer.

"I will take care of you," said the woman. "You may rest on my walking stick for the journey."

So Sid agreed. Off together, the unlikely pair traveled. With her black shawl draped across her head and penetrating, coal black eyes, the old crone looked like a crow herself. They traveled the forest for many days. They quenched their thirst at little streams. Sid picked the last of this year's berries because the gnarled fingers of his friend weren't able to grasp them. They talked and talked along the way, a little crow pouring his heart out to the only one who ever listened and cared about what he had to say.

Soon, they reached a village. The villagers yelled at the old woman to get away. They threw stones and sticks at her and at the mangy, little crow by her side. Sid hid under her shawl; never was he so afraid.

The old woman tumbled and fell, the final stone hitting her forehead. And there they left her. The villagers walked away laughing. Sid cried for her to awaken, but she stayed very still. It was getting dark. The villagers were gone, tucked away in warm cottages. In the cold stood a tiny crow, tears falling down his cheek.

"I cannot stay here, my friend," he cried. "Or they will kill me, too. I am just an old crow. My life is worth nothing to them. My life has been worth nothing to anyone except you, and now I must leave you alone in the road. I am sorry, my friend," he cawed mournfully.

With that, Sid plucked out one of his sparse feathers and placed it in her hand. "Remember me, for I will see you again," he cawed. "Crows always recognize a friend. We never forget. One day, above the clouds, I will see you again."

With that, Sid flew as far as his tired body could carry him into the trees. It was winter. Food was scarce. Sid grew very fragile and weak. Soon, he could not muster the strength to travel down for water or food any longer.

One night, under a full moon, Sid knew his night's dreams would be his last. As he started to close his heavy eyes, he saw a shimmering light. Within the light was a beautiful Angel, with the largest feathered wings he had ever seen. She had a kind face, with eyes that seemed familiar. Sid always recognized faces. He didn't know her, did he?

As she came closer, the Angel held out her hand. In it was one black feather, a thin feather, sparse and worn. "Come, Sid, it is time to go home. Crows never forget, and neither do old crones who become beautiful Angels in Heaven. From now on, you shall be called Obsidian, for a majestic crow is worthy of a beautiful name."

With that, she reached out to the majestic crow, now laden with ebony feathers that shimmered in the moonlight. Together, they soared above the clouds.

Fairy Vacations

Did you ever wonder

Where the fairies and the fey

Decide upon vacation

When they want to get away?

They travel down to middle earth

In deep caves out of sight

They swim in ancient lakes

They stroll in dim starlight

On furry voles they sit atop

On fuzzy bats they glide

Deep into the caverns

Deep into mountainsides

Voles carry them in tunnels

Upon bats' backs they soar

To moss-filled rooms

And crystal lakes

And cavern fairy doors

Fireflies are lanterns

Off-season time they spend

Among the fairy patrons

Their light source

They do lend

They mountain climb

Stalagmites

With rose thorns on their shoes

To grip the mighty crystals

Sparkling in the moonlit dew

They bungee jump off of

Stalactites

With dandelion chutes

They land among the soft moss

And furry cave plant roots

Where only moonlight

Glitters

They dine by sparkling ponds

On mushroom soup

And salads

Comprised of ferny fronds

And each one leaves a token

In payment to the earth

A gift of silver, gold, or jewel

In gratitude for mirth

So when you touch a ring

Of gold

Or a silver pendant fair

Or gaze upon a diamond

That sparkles on the wearer

Think of a little fairy

Who left it

Deep inside

A place of fun and laughter

Within a deep cave side

Stars

*a*braham was a tailor. He lived with his son Eli in a small village. Eli went to school while Abraham sewed coats for wealthy men. Men perhaps not as learned as Abraham, but men granted the wealth in money that Abraham and Eli possessed in love.

Each night, Abraham and Eli shared a humble dinner. When Eli's schoolwork was finished, the two of them would venture out into the night. Abraham bundled Eli in the warm coat he had sewn, and together, they walked to a nearby hill under the stars.

Eli loved the stars. Abraham knew all the constellations. He had learned them from his father, and his father had learned them from his father before him.

"Show me Cassiopeia again, papa," Eli would happily shout.

"Ah, the beauty in the sky," his father replied. "She is there, watching. Look opposite her and see the Big Dipper, my son. He is guiding many home as we watch."

"Father, are these stars really gone?" Eli asked.

"Yes, my son. They died millions of years ago, but they still bring light upon our earth."

So many stars, and such a tired, little boy. Eli would grow drowsy each night, sometimes having to be carried back home in his father's arms. Each day followed much like the same. On moonlit nights, the pair would always be stargazing.

"Is momma in the stars, papa?"

"Yes," Abraham would answer. "She is watching down over us. At night, she rides on Pegasus, the winged horse, and visits all the twinkling places in the Universe," Abraham whispered.

"Will she take us with her one day?" little Eli asked.

"Yes, one day, but not for a very long time, my son," his father answered.

And so the days continued. Father and son sharing the earth, the stars, and the Universe together each night.

Soon, Eli began to notice the streets growing emptier and emptier. "It is the cold," his father replied. "People don't want to be out in the cold night. To most, gazing at the stars is foolish."   Eli believed his father, but he still noticed the hurriedness in his steps and the tenseness in the hands that held onto his.

One afternoon, Eli came home to a very early supper. Papa wasn't at his tailor's sewing machine, which was unusual. "Come eat, then finish your schoolwork," Abraham told his son.

"Then we will go find Orion tonight," Eli answered.

"No, not tonight," Abraham sighed.

"Why, papa? Are you not feeling well?"

"Do not ask questions. Eat your supper," Abraham chastised. "I am sorry," his father added. "You are a special little boy, my son. The brightest star in all my Universe. One day, your light shall shine as brightly as Polaris."

Eli finished his supper and went to his room. Before long, he fell asleep. But Abraham did not sleep. By a dim light, he worked, his tear-filled eyes sewing a tiny, yellow star to the front of Eli's warm coat.

As he stitched, he looked out the window, trying to find Pegasus in the sky.

Acorns

*A*nnie and her grandpa loved to walk the woods beside his cottage. Each leaf, each seed, each pinecone was a treasure. Sometimes, precious butterfly wings and bird feathers lay on the ground, waiting to be scooped up into Annie's pocket.

Acorns are filled with magick, Annie's grandpa always told her. *Keep an acorn in your pocket, and magick will always be part of your day.* Annie always kept an acorn in her pocket. She pressed leaves and wildflowers, and she turned seeds and acorns into little animals and fairies.

But girls grow up and leave the woods behind for the lights of big cities, universities, and jobs. Grandpa walked the woods alone these days, looking at all the wonders that made a little girl's eyes grow wide with excitement. He kept an acorn in his pocket to remember her. Sometimes, he mailed a tiny feather or flower in a letter and wished he could see her face as she opened it.

One autumn day, Grandpa fell ill while walking in the woods. His wife found his body among the leaves and acorns. Annie came home for the service. Grandpa was laid to rest on a quiet hill in the sunshine.

Annie took out an acorn from the pocket of her coat.

"Look, Grandpa, I never forgot," she whispered. With her hands, she scooped a tiny hole in the freshly moved earth. "One day, Grandpa, a tree full of magick will tower over your head. Each acorn that falls to the earth will be a moment when I think of you and all the wondrous memories you have given to me."

As she walked from the grave, Annie's foot crunched on something hard on the ground. Could it be? Annie recognized that crunch. It was an acorn, but there were no trees around.

"Thanks, Grandpa," she whispered. Then, Annie placed the acorn inside her coat pocket.

Church Mouse Christmas

Collin was a little church mouse. He lived in a beautiful cathedral, filled with magnificent statues and flickering candles.

Each day, Collin slept in a tiny mouse hole in the nave. His tiny mouse snores were drowned out by the pipes of the church organ and the ringing of the cathedral bells. But each night, Collin would have the whole cathedral to himself. Well, almost to himself, for there were many other little church mice who called it home.

Collin's favorite time of year was Christmas. Scents of incense and pine wafted through the massive halls, and festive lights twinkled among the beams of each rafter. Comfy straw was placed inside a beautiful manger. Collin stuffed a bit each night into his whiskered cheeks and carried it to his mouse bed. It was so warm and snuggly.

The cathedral held many special services during this time, some at night, so Collin had to be extra quiet. Collin's favorite service was one just before Christmas Day. After Mass, the church volunteers held a bake sale to raise money to keep the cathedral looking beautiful. Collin loved the bake sale. People always dropped crumbs outside the cathedral. It was a feast for a little mouse. Teacakes and scones and mincemeat pies—all things to make a little mouse's mouth water. Collin made endless trips to and from the path of crumbs until his winter storehouse was laden with all sorts of confections.

Christmas night, when all humans were tucked away in bed, Collin and the other church mice gathered for their own feast. Tiny tablecloths lined the kneeling benches; tiny goblets of water gleaned from the baptismal font sparkled in the candlelight. Tiny pillows stuffed with nativity straw set the place for each cathedral mouse.

But then, the most wondrous thing happened. It happened every year.

They came. The stray rats, the pigeons, the foxes, the skunks, the field mice, the feral cats, the little voles, the sparrows. They came. They crawled in tiny holes; they slid through little cracks; they flew through holes in leaking rafters. All sat beside the kneeling benches, all placed tiny paws on sparkling goblets, and all laid their tired heads on pillows of straw.

And then they left before the morning light of Christmas Day. Not a crumb remained, not a snippet of straw, not a trace to be seen by any who came to Mass that day— except for the tiny baby in the manger of straw who welcomed them all, each tired, hungry mouth.

And, as Collin snored quietly, yet one more wondrous thing happened. His little mouse storehouse of sweet confections overflowed with plenty, more than enough to last throughout the harsh winter.